NAUGHTY NINJA
TAKES A BATH

By **TODD TARPLEY**   Illustrated by **VIN VOGEL**

two lions

A special thanks to Merideth, Kelsey, and my agent, Teresa Kietlinski. —V. V.

Published by Two Lions, New York

www.apub.com

Amazon, the Amazon logo, and Two Lions are trademarks of Amazon.com, Inc., or its affiliates.

ISBN-13: 9781542094337
ISBN-10: 154209433X

The illustrations were created digitally.

Book design by AndWorld Design
Printed in China

First Edition

10 9 8 7 6 5 4 3 2 1

For Jo—T. T.

To Ricardo and my goddaughter, Marie—V. V.

Naughty Ninja emerged from the jungle after a long day of training.

He was covered with river mud, smelly leaves, and beetle dung. Flies buzzed around him.

Crossing one last raging river in his backyard, he entered his secret ninja training camp.

"NAUGHTY NINJA NEEDS FOOD!"
he announced.

"*Pee-yew*, Will!" said Dad.
"First you need a bath."

"And then we'll have ninja
nuggets for lunch,"
Mom added.

"Now, Will, you're going to take a bath calmly," said Dad.

"And whatever you do, you're not going to say 'Ninja to the rescue!' Whenever you say that, something bad happens."

But Naughty Ninja wasn't paying attention. The flies that had been buzzing around him were now buzzing around his dad.

Naughty Ninja suddenly realized they were wild, poisonous flies from the jungle. He quickly hatched a plan.

"Don't say 'Ninja to the rescue,'" pleaded Dad. "Please don't say 'Ninja to the rescue.'"

"NINJA TO THE RESCUE!"

shouted Naughty Ninja.

"NOOOO!" cried Dad in slow motion.
But Naughty Ninja was too fast.

Naughty Ninja wondered why Dad was in the bathtub with his clothes still on. A wild, angry alligator must have pulled him in!

"Is Ninja Dad okay?" he asked.

"Ninja Dad does not want to be in
the tub," said Dad, trying to sound calm.
"Ninja Dad wants you in the tub."

BUBBLE
BATH

Naughty Ninja quickly hatched a plan.

"NINJA TO THE RESCUE!"

he shouted.

"NOOOO!" Dad cried in slow motion.
But Naughty Ninja was too fast.

Water was everywhere . . . on the ceiling, on the walls, and all over the floor.

But the coast was clear. Naughty Ninja had saved his dad.

"Is Ninja Dad better now?" he asked.

"Actually, no," said Dad,
squeezing water from his clothes.
"Ninja Dad is *not* better."

Naughty Ninja wondered what Dad meant. Naughty Ninja had rescued him from wild, poisonous flies and a wild, angry alligator.

If Dad was still in trouble, it could only mean one thing . . .

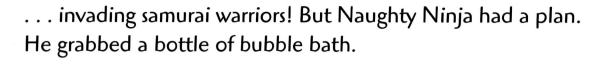. . . invading samurai warriors! But Naughty Ninja had a plan. He grabbed a bottle of bubble bath.

"NINJA TO THE RESCUE!"

he shouted.

"NOOOO!" cried Dad in slow motion.
But Naughty Ninja was too fast.

Bubbles quickly filled the tub and spilled onto the floor.

In a matter of seconds, they filled the entire bathroom.

"Run, Ninja Dad!"
shouted Naughty Ninja.
"RUN!"

Naughty Ninja jumped from the tub to the toilet seat,
to the sink, and out the door, with bubbles close behind.

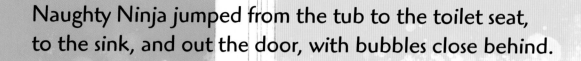

Dad grabbed an armful of towels and ran after him.

"Will, stop!" wailed Dad.
"You're making a huge mess!"

Then Dad slipped, landed on a towel, and went sliding across the room. He bounced off a wall, then slid back across the floor in the other direction.

"WHOOOOA!"

Naughty Ninja thought that looked like fun.

"WHEEEE

So he slid across the room too,
around all four walls—even the ceiling.

"YIPPPEEE!" cried Dad, suddenly having fun.

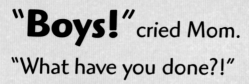

"Boys!" cried Mom.

"What have you done?!"

Naughty Ninja and
Dad stopped and slowly
pointed at each other.

"Never mind who did what," said Mom, hugging them both. "Thank you for cleaning the house! It looks spotless."

Naughty Ninja looked around the room. It *was* spotless. All that soapy water had actually cleaned it up.

"Well, you know what
we ninjas like to say," Dad said
and winked at Will.

"NINJA TO THE RESCUE!"

shouted Naughty Ninja.

And, once again,
the world was saved.

At least for the next hour.